DOUBTFUL TALES DOUBTFUL TALES
DOUBTFUL TALES DOUBTFUL TALES
DOUBTFUL TALES DOUBTFUL TALES
DOUBTFUL TALES DOUBTFUL TALES
DOUBTFUL TALES DOUBTFUL TALES
DOUBTFUL TALES DOUBTFUL TALES
DOUBTFUL TALES DOUBTFUL TALES
DOUBTFUL TALES DOUBTFUL TALES
DOUBTFUL TALES DOUBTFUL TALES
DOUBTFUL TALES DOUBTFUL TALES
DOUBTFUL TALES DOUBTFUL TALES
DOUBTFUL TALES DOUBTFUL TALES
DOUBTFUL TALES DOUBTFUL TALES
DOUBTFUL TALES DOUBTFUL TALES

DOUBTFUL TALES DOUBTFUL TALES
DOUBTFUL TALES DOUBTFUL TALES
DOUBTFUL TALES DOUBTFUL TALES
DOUBTFUL TALES DOUBTFUL TALES
DOUBTFUL TALES DOUBTFUL TALES
DOUBTFUL TALES DOUBTFUL TALES
DOUBTFUL TALES DOUBTFUL TALES
DOUBTFUL TALES DOUBTFUL TALES
DOUBTFUL TALES DOUBTFUL TALES
DOUBTFUL TALES DOUBTFUL TALES
DOUBTFUL TALES DOUBTFUL TALES
DOUBTFUL TALES DOUBTFUL TALES
DOUBTFUL TALES DOUBTFUL TALES
DOUBTFUL TALES DOUBTFUL TALES

1st Edition

www.cvdarts.com
cvdarts@hotmail.com
markfribbensauthor@gmail.com

Intr...Introd.....The Basics

The Tales you are about to be told have reached this planet via an incredibly complicated computer set up, that I don't really understand.
Their accuracy is certainly in question, but we think that on the whole they're probably nonsense.
From the Planet Tradagon, not that dissimilar to Earth, in a Parallel Universe in the Wotsit Nebula, comes the Tale of Sebastian Headline.
He is known as the man with an ear for a story, and these are the latest News and features obtained from his broadcasts. The language is predominantly English, with recognisable similarities to things on Earth, but there is a Tradagon dictionary section at the end of the book to help.

Final Warning
This really isn't for kids.

Dedicated to
Searchers of knowledge and
Historical events, fabricated within
the mind of
A nutter.

SEBASTIAN HEADLINE

REPORT ONE

From Sebastian Headline
Live from the Tradagon
Newsroom.

BONG !

Celebrity Gardener, Tarty Hanglow, in
Bongo disaster

BONG !

Phantom Cereal Wedger strikes again

BONG !

Primal Minster disappears up his own
Buggerbox.

Good morrow Tradagon, here are your headlines.

 **Celebrity Gardener, Tarty Hanglow**, was last night being questioned by the Siren Bobby Men, following an accident on the set of her new Television Show, 'Garden Wobblers'.

It appears that during shooting, Tarty, famous for not wearing a bongo sling, popped out as she swung around, knocking a small child flying with her left bongo.

The young lad, Podrich 7, was said to be comfortable in hospital, but suffering with wobbler whiplash. His dad, Randy said,

"If it had been me I would have fuckin loved it, but Poddy is too small to cope with that much flesh in the face."

Tarty was unavailable for comment, but her

spokesperson said,

"Tarty was very upset by the incident, but the simple fact is, she never wears a bongo sling because she loves the feel of her tops rubbing against her nudge wizzlers.

Of course she feels for the lad and has sent him a gift of two large peaches to cheer him up."

Randy had asked for a photo of her twadge, but Tarty declined.

The Phantom Cereal Wedger has struck again, claiming his ninth victim. Yesterday the chief of Siren Bobby Men, CSI Ewesliss, confirmed that they are no closer to catching the fiend who has terrorised the public for months.

His latest victim, Tony Tonka, was said to be bending down, tying his shoo leads in Hydey Park, when suddenly his bot snugglers were wrenched up and filled with coco flakes. Luckily he managed to escape before the milk could be added.

Chief Ewesliss said,

"It's a worrying trend. The Phantom is very clever. He catches his victims at weak moments then disappears into the shadows. But I've got a good team and I'm sure that one of these days we'll get him."

Mr Tonka was distraught, and said it took over an hour to get all the flakes out, some of which had gone down to his ankles. And his wife was demanding to know if his flapping bot snugglers smelling of coco, was an attempt to attract hungry tramps.

The story did have a happy ending though, as amongst all the flakes, Mr Tonka found a small golden envelope containing a, 'Kids go free' voucher for Willy Wanka Land.

**There were dramatic scenes at Worstminster yesterday**, when during a fierce bout of questions from opposition leader, Dwain Cameltoe, The Primal Minster, Royston Beige, suddenly disappeared up his own buggerbox, and refused to come out until,

"All the nasty men had gone away."

Mr Beige, who is due to meet with Sarah Sniff today, to put the final touches to his sneezing tax, was last night said to be still up there, with only one hand popping out to operate the TV remote control. His Mum said,

"Unless the boys decide to play nicely, my Royston refuses to come out. There are a lot of bullies at Worstminster, and I think they should be sent home to have a jolly good think about their behaviour."

Of course this isn't the first time Mr Beige has acted strangely when feeling under pressure. Two years ago he smashed a dozen cluck orbs over his head before going on a public walk to save time.

Mr Beige has so far refused to comment.

MORE NEWS STORIES LATER........

And now for all you nature lovers, here is a special feature from, PERCY TWITCHER.

He Observes, and Tries to Re-inact the actions of Nature's Creatures

(Please use Australian Accent when reading this Feature.)

Hello Nature Lovers, I just love this time of year. There's nothing quite like going into the countryside and dipping your schnoozle...

Not of course to the extent of the nudelites who run around with their ram danglers hanging out. I mean simply to observe and re-inact the wonders of the natural world.

Last weekend was such a time. My team and I had been exploring the Vestian Plains near Crumpsing, when we discovered a very rare and beautiful flapper, known locally as a Twoddle Puffer.

Now apart from its wonderfully colourful flappage and rather large grill poker, this amazing creature has the ability to attract potential mates, by whistling through its klunge flaps.

As you well know, my task is to observe and re-inact the actions of the countryside creatures. So later that evening, after we had set up camp and lit a fire, I decided to have a go at attracting a potential mate of my own by whistling through my very own flaps.

First, I lowered my bot snugglers. Then rocking onto my back, with my legs a kimbo, I attempted the whistling task. I'll be honest, it was a fuckin disaster. I'd been mainly eating berries and beans all day and had little or no control over my flaps nor the pressure required.

Not only did the discharge sound more like an untied balloon being released into the air, but it also mixed with the open fire, causing an explosion that blew the fuckin tents away. And the aroma was enough to cause all my buddies to leave camp as quickly as possible. So instead of being an attraction, it was more of a repellent.

However, much to my amazement, my old drinking pals, Tommy Twang and Gary Snutch, turned up out of the blue, saying that they would recognise that sound anywhere !!

I hadn't seen them since we'd been on the channel 46 TV Show, 'The Shat Busters' together. So despite the fact that my task had completely failed, it was great to catch up with my old buddies again.

Well I'll see ya next time folks, till then, dip your schnoozle and enjoy the wonders of nature.

And now a segment from Tradagon's Global History Department, Obtained from Another Planet.

LADY FAULKINGTON-BATTERMORE'S DIARY

Lady Faulkington-Battermore is so posh she can hardly talk. When reading her diary it is advised that you adopt a very posh, elderly accent

Hello there, my name is Lady Faulkington-Battermore, and I'm so posh, I can hardly talk.

This is my Diary of the day.

This morning, I asked for some decorators to frequent the house in order to supply me with a quote for some restoration work in the drawing room.

Unfortunately, when they arrived, I simply had no choice but to send them away again, because quite frankly it was clearly obvious that they were working class, and they offended my eyes. Not a cravat or double breasted coat in sight. Instead an item of clothing I believe was referred to as a, 'Bib and Brace', something that you would expect a clown to wear. I'm surprised that when they drove away in their cheap little clown car, that one of the doors didn't fall off.

I required a schooner of sherry to calm my nerves.

This afternoon, a lady of somewhat reduced breeding stopped me outside one of the town's luxurious department stores. Apparently she was conducting some survey or another on the shopping habits of the modern woman.

I was naturally polite, but informed her that it was not possible for me to answer any questions from a lady wearing imitation earrings.

Having suggested that perhaps she would be better off selling small pieces of heather, I swished my Pashmina into her inexperienced face, and headed straight for Country Casuals.

I spent the evening in the cocktail lounge of the Royal Albert Hotel, where having clasped an aperitif from a charming waiter with a silver tray, my eyes were suddenly offended by a ghastly little man wearing a quite revolting Hawaiian shirt.

He was introduced to us as the Disc Jockey, and he asked if we might have any requests for him. I said,

"Yes, go and change that ridiculous shirt. I hardly think that palm trees and coconuts are quite the Royal Albert."

He replied,

"Yo respect in da house, you is wicked doll."

I told him to bugger off.

I retired to my Lola Ashmillon, furnished boudoire at five and twenty to eleven. Once there I showered for a little over 45 minutes, in an attempt to wash the lower classes from my body.

LADY FAULKINGTON-BATTERMORE'S TIP OF THE DAY

Although, on the whole, birds are quite delightful creatures with their graceful movement and angelic song, you do not want the buggers nesting up in the eaves of your house, pooping on your Bentley or designer hat.

To solve this problem, simply instruct your groundsman or gardener to place several cats into baby bouncers and attach them to the gutters around your building.

The sight of the bouncing felines should keep the birds well away, although the odd stubborn one, might poop themselves a bit more than usual before they depart.

Thank you so much for your very kind attention, and felicitations to all of you.

Lady FB.

On Tradagon we are very proud of our culinary expertise. With some of the very best chefs in the sector, living right here on the planet. One of the most well known is **Bernie Lott**. Although somewhat rude, his recipes and skills are second to none.

BERNIE LOTT
With one of his
Favourite dishes.
**Roast Frazzle nosed
Wam Schniggler
With Seasonal
Grollysquats**

Right, you bunch of fuckin nookies, as you're here you might as well learn something, yes?

This is one of the most popular dishes on Tradagon. It's so easy, even a redbot fluff mongler could prepare it.

First, you get your Wam Schniggler. You could buy a middle joint at the Carniboshers, but personally I much prefer to buy baby ones as pets. Then get my kids to name them, help rear them and fall in love with them. Then while the kids are at school, I slaughter them and get the kids a long eared sniffer instead.

Which reminds me, we may well be featuring long eared sniffer stew next time.

Right, let's begin, yes? Firstly, shove your joint into a plopper. Cover with clear juice and allow to soak for 8 to 10 nodes. Then change the juice and lose the sawty.

Scringe, and add new clear juice. Bring to the fartel and get rid of the shat. Then lower the heat and cover the plopper.

Burple slowly, allowing half a node per 500g, scringe and slightly cool. Don't over burple or it will come out looking like a fuckin wrinkler's arse.

Strip the fleshty off and score the flabbage into diamond shapes with a sharp Kniffle.

Press a waj pizzle into each alternate diamond and place joint in a roasting comodal.

OK, coating time.

NO !! we are not going to open a fuckin jar of Pecker tonight, we're gonna make our own.

First, combine sweet grain with bee splurge, melted churney, scrumpy juice and twizzler sauce, yes? Then coat the scored flabbage with the mixture.

Cook in the centre of a moderately hot baker box for half a node or so, basting with splodge 3 or 4 times till golden brown.

Today's seasonal grollysquats are:

New tattage, which can be either fartled or part fartled, then coated with sea sawty and rhyme and added to the baker box prior to the Wam schniggler. Or fartled along with, pop on the nob, baby schnozzles and fresh, green pod rollers.

Then Scringe and serve with generous slices of the sauce covered meat.

Frazzle Nosed Wam schniggler with seasonal grollysquats...DONE.

Now fuck off out of my kitchen !!!!!

REPORT TWO
From Sebastian Headline
Live from the Tradagon
Newsroom.

BONG !

Man in Bournegob voted unluckiest man in
Tradagon, after his flapper encounters.

BONG !

Teacher from the Rookie mountains makes
embarrassing mistakes on her Job Application.

A man from Bournegob has Been voted this year's unluckiest man, by the readers of 'You poor Bastard' Magazine, after he has been flan shittled on 68 times by flappers.

Roy Cardigan of Hitchcock Lane, Bournegob, has been hit with flan shittle about every 5 days during this year.

It doesn't seem to matter where he goes or what he does, the flapper fiends always seem to be close by.

He recalls the first of the year was when he was lake fishing with his good friend, Tom Thick.

"We were pitched on the river bank, and we hadn't had a nibble in ages, when all of a sudden my line started to pull and I knew I had hooked a gilly slip, and by the pull, it seemed a big one. I was excited as I pulled backwards and forwards while reeling him in.

Unfortunately, as sometimes happens, the line snapped and I fell onto my back with my face in the air. It was at that very second that a flapper released its load all over my grill. I can remember screaming like a klunge and diving in the lake to wash it off."

On another occasion, he and Tom were feeding seals at the zoo with seafood when another flapper struck. Here's Tom Thick with the story.

"Roy n that....It were poop...ehh?"

Ok well perhaps Roy should tell us the story.

"Tom and I were holding out small gilly slips from a cup to feed the seals at Bournegob Zoo, when all of a sudden a blasted flapper flew down and stole the gilly slip from my hand. But not content with that, he then landed on my head, flan shittled, and flew off! I yelled and ran to the public loos to clean up."

I think it's fair to say that Roy has certainly suffered quite a lot of distress due to the flappers.

But there was one occasion when Roy actually admired what had happened. Here's his story.

Tom and I were bombing down the freeway in my car. It was a lovely summer's day and I had the sun roof open. We were laughing and singing along to the music on the radio when all of a sudden a shitlet landed in my lap. I couldn't believe it! But as I thought about it, I realised that in order to get me through the sun roof, that flapper would have had to take into consideration the height he was flying, the speed I was travelling and the timing to release. I must admit, on that one occasion, I had to give it to the little fucker, that was some shot!"

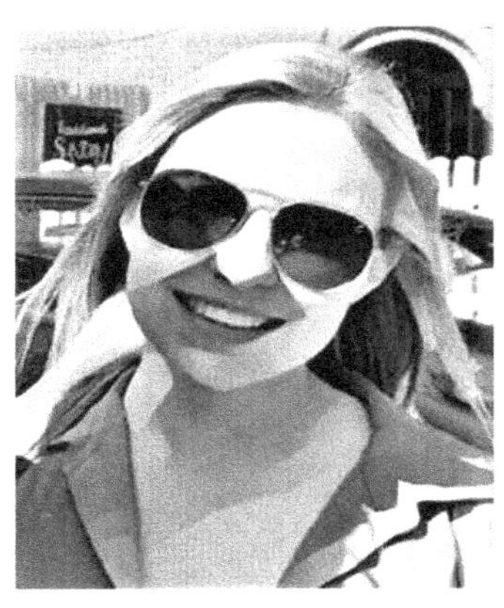

A Teacher from the Rookie Mountains area has embarrassed herself when submitting her application for a new teaching position.

Linda Con-fuse, a qualified and experienced teacher from the Rookie Mountains area, enjoys her job very much as a teacher, working her way up from kinder garden to secondary education and even running a school. However, Mrs Con-fuse, along with her husband are also members of the Tradagon swingers club, and often enjoy weekends away in the country to pursue their adult activities.

Unfortunately, having arrived home late on the Sunday night, Linda had forgotten that she had to get her job application in by first thing on the Monday morning for a new school position and had yet to write it. So in the early hours, while feeling sleepy and still excited from her weekend away, she decided to compile the letter.

The following two passages are from the application she wanted to send to the Head governor of the posh school she was applying for. And from the application she actually sent them.....

Passage from the application she wanted to send:

Dear Professor Wagstaff,

When people ask me what my favourite occupation is, I always say I love to be teaching. And it would be an honour to teach the over sixteens if duly appointed.

I enjoy relaxing pastimes like yoga and jogging, and have always been a calm person. While I viewed many other teachers in stress, I would simply be sitting quietly in the staff room or library without any issues at all.

I never shy away from awkward young adults, I steer them away from bad habits and like to show them just how accommodating my class can be. And when we put a super presentation together, there's nothing I like more than showing my class off in assembly for the rest of the school to admire.

I'm never afraid of hard jobs, and have worked my way up the ranks to becoming head. Although this position is perhaps a step down, I always get on well with teachers and pupils alike and have met some great characters along the way.

I recall an A level student called Laura. She and her friends were a little worried when I put them into the top bracket for Maths. But I was confident and told them that if anyone could, I figured her and her friends could.

My favourite teacher was the nutty music teacher, John Lovett. During exams he always got his silver clock out and placed it on the front desk for all to see. He taught me a lot about teaching and when I left, I thanked him for all I had learnt.

Well anyway, I very much hope to receive an interview and look forward to seeing you then.
Yours Sincerely
Linda Con-Fuse.

Passage from the application she actually sent:

Dear Professor Wankstain,

When people ask me what my favourite penetration is, I always say I love to be screeching. And it would be an honour to teach the over sexed teens if double jointed.

I enjoy relaxing pastimes, like yoga and dogging, and have always been a calm person. While I viewed many other teachers in stress, I would simply be shitting quietly in the staff room or library without any tissues at all.

I never shy away from awkward young adults, I steer them away from bad rabbits and like to show them just how accommodating my arse can be. And when we put a super presentation together, there's nothing I like more than showing my arse off in assembly for the rest of the school to admire.

I'm never afraid of hand jobs, and have worked my way up the wanks to giving head. Although this position is perhaps a step down, I always get on well with teachers and pupils alike and have met some great characters along the way.

I recall an A level student called Laura. She and her friends were a little worried when I put them into the top bracket for Maths. But I was confident and told them that if anyone could, I fingered her and her friends good.

My favourite teacher was the nutty music teacher, John Lovett. During exams he always got his shiny cock out and placed it on the front desk for all to see. He taught me a lot about teaching and when I left, I wanked him for all I was worth.

Well anyway, I very much hope to receive an interview and look forward to seeing you then.
Yours Sincerely
Linda Con-Fuse.

Needless to say, not only did she not get an interview but she was also reported to the authorities and had a jolly hard time explaining the truth..

MORE NEWS STORIES LATER.

**And Now to our latest
Story from Office Jane,
And her Idiot Manager**

"More tea Vicar," I jokingly said, as my manager, Daniel Wafter, broke wind for the fifth time in as many minutes.

The comical line was wearing a bit thin, but then so was the level of oxygen in the room. Of course it was mainly due to his love of beetroot and radishes. In fact, apart from the odd cream bun sneaked into the office on one of the staff birthdays, his entire diet consisted of fresh fruit and grollysquats.

This had started since Bernie Lott had mentioned on his television programme, 'Won't Cook Can't be Fuckin Arsed' that you should always have a good helping of both each day.

Of course trying to point out that Bernie had meant along with other foods, was a pointless exercise.

I sat and watched as he scribbled erratically over several papers in writing that his secretary would have absolutely no chance of reading, and I realised something.
He didn't even realise that he had sent for me, or indeed that I had even entered the room, despite my Vicar quip.

I didn't dislike Daniel and he was certainly a nice enough person, but I couldn't help thinking, 'He's a bit of a thicky'. A huge smile came to my face as I thought how wonderful it must be to be a bit thick.

All the worries and troubles of the world wouldn't bother you, because they would simply go over your head. And hardly anyone could upset you, because quite frankly you never listened to them.

My thoughts were disturbed by yet another break of wind...

"Is it ok if I open a window?" I asked politely.

Daniel was obviously startled by my request, as well as the fact that I was in his office in the first place.

"I should think so too, the way you're going on!" he replied.

It was at that point that I remembered that another part of a thicky's personality was complete denial and buck passing wherever possible.

"You'll need the key...It's in the wotsit," he added, pointing towards a blank wall.

I desperately started to look around the room for something that might be wotsit shaped, but I was in a race against time. The air was thinning and the next 'Dan Flan' was no doubt already brewing.

I frantically searched in all the containers, cups, boxes and drawers that I could see, while pinching my nose.

I knew that asking Daniel would be like asking a chimpanzee to explain the theory of relativity. In fact I would be surprised if he even dressed himself in the morning.

I had to face it, I was on my own and I was starting to panic, in case someone walked in with a lit cigarette and blew us all away.

"Have you found it yet Judy? He asked without looking.

"It's Jane, Mr Wafter, Jane," I remarked.

Suddenly I found the key. It was in the window handle where I had first headed. I quickly opened the window and the fresh air began to fill my lungs. Daniel walked up to the window beside me.

"You really are a smelly bitch, Joice"

"It's Jane Sir."

"Whatever."

I had no idea what a wotsit was or what Daniel had put inside it, and I didn't care that he got my name wrong and even blamed me for the smell. The fact is, I could breathe again, and life was good.

On the planet Tradagon, the world
Of Entertainment is a very
important part of our recreational
life, so this feature is vital to give
you the up to date news.

ENTERTAINMENT
WITH
MEL SWINGER

Hi guys,

Welcome to my Entertainment section, featuring

Film reviews, televison, books and celebrities.

FILM REVIEWS

'HEDGE YOUR BETS'

This Adam Bleacher film sees Shoo shop worker, Simon Balls, disguise himself as a small privet hedge, in order to get closer to the love of his life, Sally Flange, played by the delightful Cortina Ford.

After many problems With security guards and weeing dogs, Simon finally plucks up the courage to talk to Sally, who is scared shitless, by the talking evergreen. But soon she befriends it and even buys It gifts of plant food and greenfly repellent.

The slapstick is of a good quality, although the camel riding scene was a bit far fetched. But nevertheless it was a good laugh all the same.   **8/10**

'BATHAM RETURNS AGAIN LIKE BEFORE 7'

Sadly, this story starring the usually reliable Bruce Pickle, as the super hero flying Wam Schniggler is absolutely ridiculous.

Firstly, the pot bellied hero can hardly take off due to his heavy wobblers. And secondly, his arch enemy 'The Piddler' played by Jimmy Knuckleton is hardly menacing. He just goes around weeing up the back of people's coats. A very poor sequel to the original, and even the lovely Fiona Tits who plays the love interest is unable to save this Wam schniggler from the slaughter house. How Batham manages to trap The Piddler with his Ram Dangler nozzle clamp is unbelievable.

Definitely One to Miss   **2/10**

TELEVISION

This sector's Top Soap - **Holly Emmerenders street.** The plots this Sector:-

Down on the farm, Reg loses his father's watch when going elbow deep into Daisy the cow's bot during the birth of her calf.

Sally the school teacher, finds out that despite her best efforts to seduce Brandon, he still prefers to play with Ram danglers and bought himself a klunge pole to practice on.

After viewing secret papers, Curly the chef discovers that his mum, Sandra, is actually really his

Dad. His Dad Stevie is actually really his mum. His Uncle Bunny is his Aunt Mable, his Auntie Florence is really his brother. His 1st cousin Annabelle who he has been having sex with is actually his real Uncle Bunny. His cat is his dog, his dog is a goldfish, his postman is the milkman while his milkman is a TV repair girl called Betty who he married before finding out that she was actually his sister-in-law, and therefore already married.

What's been going on in the Big Brooder House?

It's been a crazy sector in the house. Here are a few of the highlights.

1 Following a tongue tizzle with Boo, Sam discovers
   That one of his bean bags is longer than the other.

2 While dancing the Canny Can, Grunt let off a Bot
   Bazooka so bad, that the house had to be
   evacuated.

3 Blossom sobs in the dreary room after one of her
   eye hedges had to be shaved off by the frilly Bot
   Snuggler wearing Dave, after she failed the task
   of making two tassels spin in opposite directions
   when attached to her Nudge wizzlers.

BOOKS
Two books that have become available from another planet in the last few sectors.

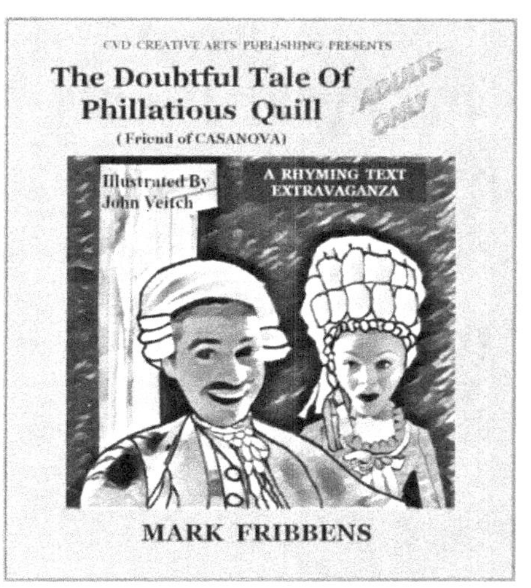

The Doubtful Tale of Phillatious Quill

An Adult Rhyming Book about the Life of Casanova's best friend and the naughty adventures they used to get up to together.
Available in Paperback and kindle from Amazon, Now.

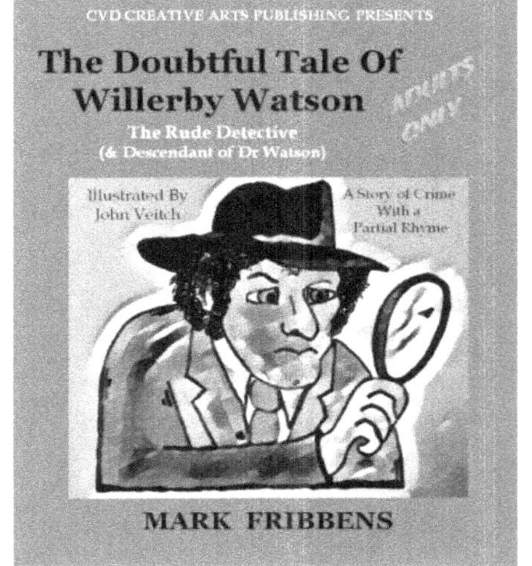

The Doubtful Tale of Willerby Watson

An Adult Tale about a Rude and junkie detective in London in the 1960's, who is trying to solve a case of a playing card serial killer.
Available in Paperback and kindle From Amazon Now.

CELEBRITY
QUICK NEWS

The brand new series of:-
"I'm a Celebrity, Quick, chuck me in the jungle cause my career is going down the Pan"
Is coming to our screens soon. And already the bursting bongo slings are being prepared for the showers.

Personally I can't wait to see this bunch of forgotten luvvies munching down on a pair of Gillyslip's peepers, or a Flapper's Twadge.

It's always a good viewing, and who knows, you might even recognise someone this time !!

That's all the Entertainment Folks,
Laters.......

Well For All You Followers of fashion, Here is a special segment from the flamboyant **RIK WANG**

FASHION TIPS
WITH
RIK WANG

Well hello there darlings, Rik Wang here, and I'm back with some absolutely fantastic fashion ideas, upcoming trends and the very best advice, in order for you to look simply fabulous during this sector.

It's been an amazing season and I've travelled far and wide to bring you the following must have items to grace any wardrobe or drawer.

We start with this absolutely sensational, Toilet pedestal head piece. Simply fluffy and scrumptious with a slight rubber backing for non slip comfort. Available in a whole host of pastel colours. With this piece of quality item, you really will be the talk of the town.

****

THIS SECTOR'S HOT FASHION TIP

Roll neck sweaters are really the thing to have during this sector's cooler weather.

Not only are they stylish and bongo hugging, they also give you a fantastic extra option...

If you have a puss podule on your face or indeed if you are just generally hideous, you can roll the neck up, right over your head !!

What a bonus yes?
Please do not forget to cut out eye holes in the neck area if you are thinking about moving around the house at all.

(Or just the one hole if you are a Cyclops !)

Now, with Purple being this sector's fashion colour, here is the latest Tradagon salon product for all you females.

PLUM HEAD
INSTANT SHAPE AND COLOUR
SALON RECOMMENDED HAIR TREATMENT

Just the thing to turn heads and get you noticed.

RIK'S SUPER SAVER SPOT

Well look at you looking all gorgeous. Without a doubt, this sector's colour is definitely purple my darlings, and your cuddly buddy, Rik, has done it again !!!

Something absolutely scrumptious with a high fashion look, at a high street price.

Fantastic accessorising using the purple and silver foil from the inside of a chocolate bar !!

Absolutely wonderful necklace, earrings, bracelet and ring set. Not just deliciously sparkling, but also giving off a slight aroma of chocolate which as we know is irresistible to millions.

See you next time guys !!!

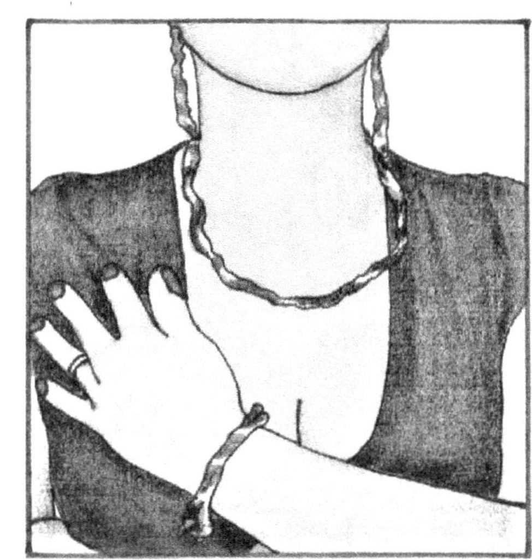

BONG !

Wrinkler still attacking youngsters in Formansdale Park.

BONG !

Butler in compromising position with Lady of the house.

This is a young man who has asked not to be recognised, who has become the latest victim of the Formansdale Park Wrinkler. He bravely recounts his harrowing story when he was attacked.

The young man was minding his own business in Formansdale Park, when he was suddenly overcome by the very strong smell of lavender.

Artists Impression Of Wrinkler

"The flowery smell was overwhelming and I felt really faint. Next thing I know I'm being held hostage in a retirement complex near Waddlepond. At first the elderly lady seemed quite pleasant, asking if I would like a hot drink. I was a little scared but thought it best to be polite, so I thanked her and asked for a coffee. I knew from her expression that I had answered incorrectly. 'I think you mean Tea!' She snapped.

Despite the fact that the temperature of her apartment was around 38 degrees, she then insisted that I put on a cardigan to keep the draft off. Again I was starting to feel faint but that was only the start of my ordeal.

I was then forced to suck a boiled sweet while watching re-runs of 'Murder she wrote' on the television. This was followed by a period drama, and a romantic Christmas film, even though it was July.

The streams of sweat were pouring down my face, and just when I thought things couldn't get any worse, she insisted that I learn how to knit a tea cosy and help her find all the edge pieces of her jigsaw puzzle.

I thought that I would never get away, but a little later on in the evening, while playing bingo and eating Eccles cakes, I said that I needed to use the bathroom, and having climbed out of the window, ran for safety.

Due to dehydration, I was unable to remember the location of the apartment, when questioned by the Siren bobby men, but I only hope that this Wrinkler is caught soon. I count myself very lucky to have survived. Her next victim might not be as fortunate."

BUTLER IN COMPROMISING POSITION WITH LADY OF THE HOUSE

Butler, Brian Smedley, had been working for Lord and Lady Dansley for only 3 years, when his loyalty was truly tested for the first time.

Lord Dansley was in his early sixties Whereas his beautiful wife was only 38, and was without doubt a very sexy lady.

It was the night of the charity Ball in Handswicke Underpotty, and Lord and Lady Dansley would be out for the evening, leaving Smedley in charge. Smedley takes up the story...

"I remember the night very well, Lord and Lady Dansley were out of the house at the Charity Ball, when suddenly they returned sooner than I had expected. However it was only Lady Dansley that had returned early.

As she came in, she slowly looked me up and down, then asked me to go to her bedroom with her. Naturally I agreed, as was my place to do so.

Once there she said, 'I'd like you to take my shoes off for me Brian'.

So I did as I was asked, then she said.

"Now I would like you to take my dress off Brian."

I felt a little awkward but she was my boss so I had to obey. Then she said,

"Now Brian, take off my bra and panties."

Well I felt very nervous indeed but again, did as I was told. Then she said,

"Right Brian.... If I ever catch you wearing my clothes again you're fired do you understand?"

I felt so ashamed, I walked naked back to my quarters and I vowed never to do it again.

MORE NEWS STORIES LATER.

And now it's time for the latest **sports news**, so let's get over to the expert reporter **Wayne Vandinkle.**

TRADAGON
SPORTS WORLD
WITH
WAYNE VANDINKLE

Hi there, Cuddly Wayne here with another roundup of International sports.

Now that the 'Five ring Festival' on Tradagon is over, it's time to concentrate on more domestic matters, and in particular, The 'Get in there Noggins' championships in Snoddlegrass.

This sector saw the exciting climax of the **Jet Engine Pogo Stick competition.**

With several competitors stuck in trees, and last year's runner up, Simon Rubber, disappearing down a manhole, it all ended in a dead heat between defending champion, Terry Springer, and Rookie Sam Orbit. So the competition had to be decided by a final Bounce off.

Despite the fact that Springer clipped a low flying plane, and Orbit had got briefly held up on a Ferris wheel, they both came bouncing down the final straight, side by side. Then showing his experience with one

almighty jet fuelled boing, Springer crossed the line first.

(Albeit 700 metres above it) to retain the Title and win Gold.

After the final, Springer heaped praise on the rookie, saying,

"Wow that lad can bounce."

Crickety now, and Pongland's fast bouncer, Martin Flingoff, had a fantastic match today, in the first Testie against Old Weeland.

Flingoff, flung a series of double strength nobblers with pace, that cut through the Old Weeland defences, knocking the stick toppers flying.

He also had several leg offs, clipped and held by the slippers.

At the end of play, Old Weeland were 53 hops for 6 plops.

Football Plus, now.

KidneyPool continue to lead the **Football Plus** premier listings, with Guychester City close behind. But all eyes Tonight will be on the local Cup clash in the capital, between West Hogs and Bumnal. This contest was due to be played in the evening, but the mothers of the Bumnal side insisted that it be brought forward, as most of the team will have school in the morning. The last time they clashed, West Hogs won by 2 goals, & 2 trys.

Current Premier listing:-

Team	Goals	Trys	Yellow Jerseys	9 Dart Finishes	Points
KidneyPool	17	11	6	3	37
Guychester City	17	9	6	3	35
West Hogs	14	10	4	2	30
Bumnal	15	9	4	2	30
Chelland	15	8	4	1	28
Titnum Hopscotch	14	7	3	2	26

Guychester Utd	14	6	4	2	26
Neverton	13	5	3	2	23
Breaster City	13	5	3	2	23
Weershit Town	2	1	0	0	3

That's all for now from the world of sport. I look forward to the next report, till then have a great time guys, and stay active.

Wayne.

DEAR IVOR
YOUR QUESTIONS ANSWERED, WITH **IVOR WHINGER**

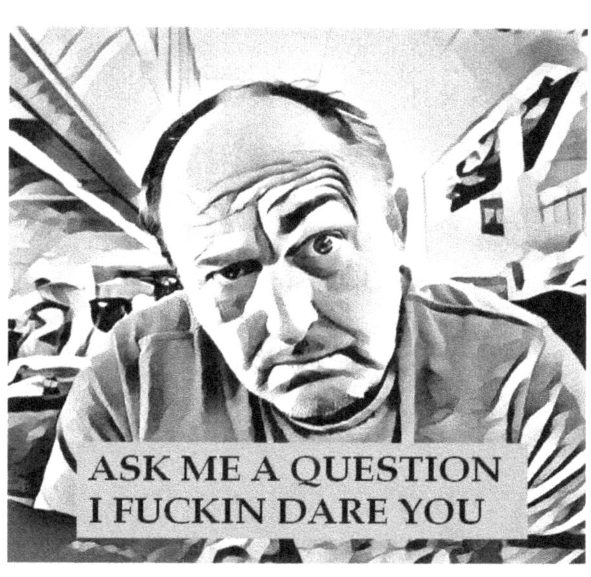

Dear Ivor,

I have led a fairly sheltered life, but having recently visited a melodic bounce station, I met a lovely Permed Sprodget, and we seemed to get on really well.

However, every time we become intimate, she seems to stop communicating and makes odd sounds.

The other night she even started to turn a funny blue colour. I am very worried that my inexperience is affecting our relationship and maybe I'm not taking the hint. How can I improve things?

Ivor Says

You soft twat, every guy remembers their first Sprodget and they can be quite difficult to handle. But your situation is very simple to rectify me old china, you're just being a muppet.

Don't forget, a Sprodget is far too polite to question her partner's sexual techniques, however despite the fact that I think you're probably fuckin useless in bed, the simple truth is that you have been holding her upside down. As for the blue colour and strange noises, you'll probably find that you were standing on her wimple tube.

Dear Ivor,

The other day, I came home to find my husband wearing my bongo sling and frilly bot snugglers, and he was prancing around the bedroom like a girl.

We had a heart to heart, and although I'm very understanding, I'm worried that he is getting very strong female tendencies and that I have lost my man forever. what can I possibly do?

Ivor Says,

Ball's in your court darling, personally I would fuck him right off, but unfortunately due to the tree huggers we must respect the sexuality of individuals and show sympathy towards their needs. However, this would be my own personal advice to you. Hold him close to you and give him a reassuring kiss on the cheek. Then having taken a step backwards, knee him as hard as you can in the crackers.

As he sinks to the floor in agony, smack him round the head with a chair and remind him that females don't have crackers, therefore, because he's in a great deal of pain, it is safe to assume that he is a man and he should fuckin start acting like one.

(We would like to point out that Ivor's views are purely his own, and would like to distance ourselves from them as much as possible and apologise to anyone who might be offended)

Dear Ivor,

I think that we are all free spirits of the land, and can make decisions for ourselves based on the Sun, Moon and natural elements of Fire, Ice, Earth, Wind and water. What do you think?

Ivor Says   Fuck off you Melt!

It's time to get technical now. One of the most fundamental and vital parts of our planet's future, is to rely on the incredible minds of our scientists and inventors. These men and women are quite determined and selfless in their pursuit of technology and finding better ways for us to function. Such a person is Professor Dilly Plonker.

PROFESSOR DILLY PLONKER'S

INVENTION FACTORY

(Scientist of the Year)
Never.....
Well, once. But only because his invention blew everyone else up.

The Amazing Flavoured Apple INVENTION

Well hello there my good friends and followers of scientific discoveries.

Over the last few months, I have been perfecting my amazing flavoured apples. It has been incredibly hard but I have now perfected my formula and can safely say I can create pretty much any flavour I wish.

To test them out, I took a batch to my local pub, 'The Dickhead's Arms', and George the Landlord said I could serve behind the bar.

After a short while, one of the locals, John, came in and asked for a Jack Daniels and coke. I said 'Right you are' and placed an apple on the bar.

'What's this?' asked John.

'Take a bite,' I said.

So he did, and a huge smile came to his face.

'Oh my god, that tastes just like Jack Daniels,' he said.

'Now turn it round and have a bite from the other side,' I said.

So he did, and again a huge smile came to his face.

'Oh my god that tastes just like coke!'

He was completely amazed and I felt good that the invention was working. Just then, another local, Peter, came up to the bar and ordered a Gin and Tonic... Once again I put an apple on the bar.

'What's this?' he said, surprised, ' I asked for a Gin and Tonic,'

'Take a bite.' Said John, smiling.

So Peter took a bite of the apple, and couldn't hide his surprise.

'Bloody hell, that tastes just like Gin.'

'Turn it round and have a bite,' said John. So Peter did, and again he laughed.

'Bloody hell, that tastes just like Tonic!'

'These are my new invention' I said. 'I reckon I can produce any flavour in the world!'

'What? Any flavour at all?' said Peter.

'Yep.'

'Alright,' said Peter grinning, 'Give me a fanny flavoured apple.'

I rummaged around, then placed an apple on the bar.

'No way!' said Peter.

'Go on, try it,' said John. So Peter did, and as he did so, he pulled a shocked face, coughed and spat the apple out on the floor.

'Fuckin Hell mate!' he shouted, 'That tastes like Shit !!'

'Turn it round,' I said.

GREAT UNCLE
BOB
TALKS
SEX

No... But erm, I'm a sensitive lover. I've been a sensitive lover all my life.

My wife once described my love making technique as shit hot. She didn't actually say the word hot, but I knew what she meant.

I think some of the stuff you youngsters get up to between the sheets is absolutely incredible. I mean, back in my day the missionary position was considered to be absolutely disgusting.

We were only allowed to perform the bayonet light bulb method. Push it in....and give it a twist.

Mind you, just lately my wife and I have started to try and rekindle things a bit. She said,

'Why don't we eat our dinner while naked tonight?' I said,

'Ok.'

So there I was sitting stark Billy Bollocks at the table, when she walked in, naked, carrying a tray. I gave her a quick look up and down and I said,

'Do you remember on our wedding night, I said that I was gonna suck your tits dry?' She said,

'Oh yes.'

I said,

' Well I was just sitting here thinking to myself, I did a bloody good job didn't I?'

Then we were half way through our starter, when she leaned across the table and said,

'Do you know something Bob, My nipples are as hot for you now as they've always been.'

I said,

'I'm not surprised, they're dangling in your soup !'

She said,

'Ohhh what's that between my breasts?'

I said,

'Your belly button!'

Then she went out and bought a pair of those crutchless knickers. You know, the ones with the hole in.

I'd never seen them before. I came in from work and there she was, spread eagled on the bed, wearing nothing but these knickers.

'Come here Bob,' she said seductively, 'I've got a surprise for you.'

I said,

'You must be joking... If it can do that to your underwear, I'm not going anywhere near it!'

Finally, we went to a local field for some nookie.

It was a field we'd visited ten years earlier. I wasted no time, I through her up against the fence and went for it. She was shaking and squirming, and her hair was all over the place. Afterwards, I said,

'I'll tell you what darling, ten years ago you never moved as well as that!'

She said,

'Ten years ago, that fence wasn't electric!'

No, but we have a laugh at the Chanctonbury. And the people here are quite friendly, you know.

One of our friends is called Maisy. She makes me laugh. She suffers from hot feet syndrome, so she decided to cut the feet off all her pairs of tights. It sounds quite sensible, but the trouble now is, every time she farts, she blows her slippers off !

Well thanks for listening to me, and I look forward to our chat next time. Till then, cheerio.....

BONG !

MODEL, SAVANA PONDA'S INFLATED LIPS, BOTH A HELP AND HINDRANCE.

BONG !

NEW VR GAME FROM TRATENDO STATION FAR TOO REALISTIC.

Model, Savana Ponda
has had a very mixed bag of
emotions lately, following
her latest cosmetic surgery.
You remember her Bot
enlargement last year,
which she had to have
reversed after getting stuck
in an elevator door.
Well she's at it again, only
this time it's her once
Perfect lips.

It seems that the inflation process was allowed to go on too long and it has left Savana with a very extraordinary look.

Unfortunately her top lip is now constantly blocking the nostrils of her nose, meaning that she has to breathe mainly through her mouth, which on occasions can give her a gormless look. Also the other day she gave her nephew a kiss and he almost lost his head.

However, as I said, there are also some upsides to the situation. When she lies down her boyfriend is delighted because he has somewhere to park his bicycle. Plus producers have been in touch with her about shooting a pilot for a new show entitled, 'A fish called Ponda.' So I guess that's pretty good.

Gaming giants, Tratendo Station, have had many calls with regard to their new VR game as it appears to be far too realistic for their customers. While playing the virtual reality game, 'Bank Robber 16,'  gamer Todd Wallaby, was actually arrested at his home in Cladderpork by the Siren Bobby Men and taken to the local station, where he was questioned for several hours about the robbery.

Across the City in Worstminster, MP Jonathan Prodder, fell asleep while playing the VR game, 'Rough Justice'. He woke up with a broken nose and a very sore bugger box.

A spokesman for Tratendo Station, Bobby Zoid, explained that their new range of games were the cutting edge of technology and these isolated incidents were just unfortunate circumstances, deriving from the truly realistic mastery of their new VR console.

Mr Zoid was later burnt at the steak having played 'Witch hunt 7 The Salem Chronicles'.

That's all the news Folks.

WEBER NUFFLER

WEBER NUFFLER'S GOT THE GEAR

Hi there Motor enthusiasts, before we start I would just like to say that 'Got the Gear' refers to great news and info regarding the world of motoring, and not something that I may or may not have in the back of my car.

Today we are featuring this little beauty.

It's called the Mantis 4000F, and it's hot off the press. When you're travelling behind some cocky twadge in a convertible, who's doing about 20 miles a node like a wrinker, cause he wants everyone to get a good look at him, you simply extend the wheel poles, and drive over the top of the Wang rubber.

And the best bit is that there's a special floor flap built in, so as you go over the top, you can drop all sorts of shit on top of him. Including the waste from your built in lavvy if you wish. Nice one guys.

According to the manual, it's also a speed monster, going from 0-60 in less than 2 secs, with a top speed of 311 miles a node. Of course the nobs stateside reckon their new motor goes from 0-60 before you've even turned on the ignition. But to be honest I think that's all a load of Bot Bazooka.

The Mantis 4000Fcomes in three metallic sprays, Slate grey, Ram Dangler Purple or Klunge Pink for the girls, and I have to say it's a joy to ride.

Here's the Latest Cars available this week.
The Mantis 4000F
The Stonka pubeflicker TSi
The Raging Hooverbag Sports
And the piece of shit from Stateside that can do one.

<u>THIS SECTORS CHERISHABLE PLATES SALE</u>

{	SH4T BOY	}	9800
{	R4MP4NT SN1FF3R	}	12300
{	W4NG RUBB3R 6	}	11900

Next time on 'Got The Gear', we feature a country car, that instead of a roof rack, has a full exterior porch complete with table & chairs and Hot tub. Mind you, watch out for those bridges!! Bye for now.

DIY WITH

MAVE
& DAVE

Alright? Today we thought we would concentrate on one of the most important aspects of the business. The practical Joke.

The following tale involves one of our

old pals Jim, who we had the pleasure of working with for some years. But first a quick bit of advice with regard to thinking on your feet.

The other day, Dave and I got to work and realised that we'd left our nosebag at home. So half way through the day we decided to get the apprentice to level the floor in the study with some self levelling compound.

We stood by the doorway and said,

"Right, if you start here and work your way over to that other door, you can open that one, and do the last square metre as you exit."

The apprentice looked across the room at the other door and smiled before mixing up the compound and starting.

Dave and I went off to strip some wallpaper in the sitting room. About half a node or so later, we returned to the door way to see that the apprentice had covered most of the floor in the thick gooey substance and was just approaching the other door.

"It's a good job there was another exit, or I would have been stuck over here in the corner," he laughed.

We laughed too, especially when he attempted to open the other door. This was because it wasn't a real exit. Dave had simply screwed a loose door to a blank wall and attached a fake handle.

The apprentice pulled at it in shock, and was gutted when he turned to see us eating his food. But it was a valuable lesson learnt. If there's no door frame, it's probably not a real door!

Anyway, back to Jim. We played what we thought would be a simple practical joke on him, which turned out to be even better that we thought.

We were working at this posh tart's house, when Jim announced that he was going to apply the brown mastic around the dark oak window in the bathroom. He got the tube out and went off to get his mastic gun.

While he popped out, we quickly removed the nozzle and stuffed some rolled up masking tape inside it before screwing it back on the tube.

Jim returned, whistling as usual, and fixed the tube to the gun. He then entered the bathroom.

We had already begun to giggle, so quietly closed the bathroom door behind him, so he couldn't hear us. We then waited for the payoff.

The surprise for us was that the posh tart came home at that very moment. She entered the hallway from the front door, and stood directly outside the bathroom door, from where Jim was starting to struggle.

Because the nozzle was blocked, he started to make all these loud straining noises, which the posh tart picked up on.

"Excuse me," she started, "But don't you have one of those portaloo thingies outside for this sort of thing?"

"Oh yes," replied Dave, "But Jim's had a bit of constipation lately, and he thought it would be too cold outside if he was struggling."

More straining noises came from the bathroom.

"Eeeeeeee...wwwoorrr..Oh come on!"

The posh tart was horrified, as Jim's groans grew louder.

"AAHHHHHHH !! Come out you fucker!"

"Look! this really isn't acceptable!!" snapped the posh tart, as Jim reached a crescendo.

WOOORR!!, Oh yes, here we go..Ahhh, AHHHHHHH, Oh God NOOO....."

There was a lot of noise and pulling of toilet roll, as the mastic tube had obviously exploded. Then suddenly the door burst open and Jim was stood there covered in brown mastic and loo paper.

"Help me guys," he said with a look of resignation on his face.

"OH MY GOD!" shouted the posh tart, just before fainting and falling on the floor.

"What's up with her?" asked Jim.

"Not sure mate," I replied. But Dave and I looked at each other and cracked up.

So remember, a practical Joke can sometimes cause a lot of trouble and you have to be prepared for that. But in this case, it went even better than planned. In fact, it was bloody brilliant!!

ANTIQUES & ART
WITH
JILLY McTART

Hello lovers of the finer things in life. Today I would like to show you two pieces that have become part of my own personal collection, and displayed at my

Studios. Firstly is this incredible piece of china ware, believe it or not, discovered at a local craft fair. I recognised its shape immediately and new the benefit of owning such a fitting piece.

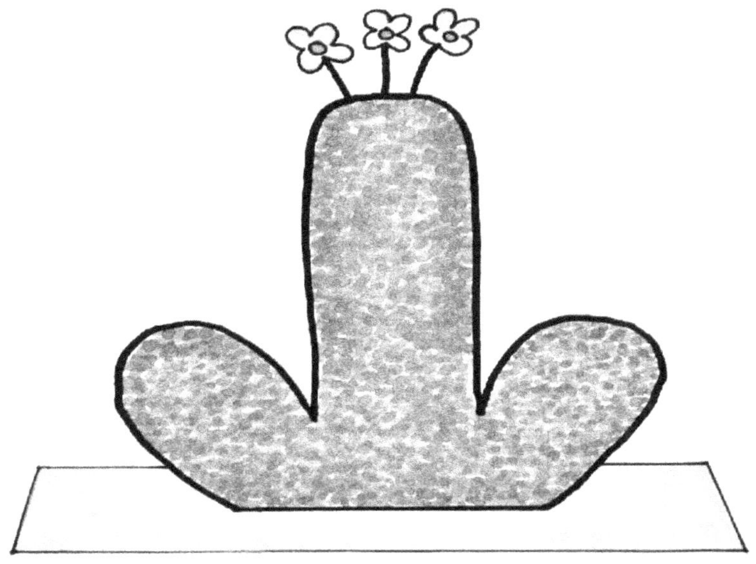

It is of course an incredible vase derived from Tagachin, and without a doubt an example of one of the finest pieces from the Wang Dynasty. I just love looking at it. It has a warmth and familiarity about it, and it feels

Great to the touch. The smooth elegant main shaft is certainly inspiring with a slightly more embossed feel to the side orbs. It really is a superbly fine Antique.

Now, moving on to Art, here is a novel piece by the Artist who brought us, 'Expressions of a Klunge'. I am of course referring to Mildred des perate.

This latest work, entitled, 'Wot no Bananas', is Mildred's inspired idea of letting a Redbot fluff Mongler loose with a canvas and paint. The results are truly amazing.

The simplistic markings, along with various adaptations of recognisable bodily parts make this quite a unique piece of work. I refer of course to the fluffy peaches, hand and facial sections which certainly enhance the overall projection. The small sections, or spots, in the top right hand corner, are believed to be poo, flung at the picture either in mischief or as a deliberate statement. (*hopefully by the hairy artist and not by anyone else*). Naturally I was more than happy to display this work in my studios, and very much look forward to Mildred's next offering,

'The Thrusting Ram Dangler'

Until next time, keep looking out for those hidden gems...

 x

HOLIDAYS & TRAVEL

With Tradagon's Favourite

Holiday Reporters

CHRISTINE TEQUILLA & FIONA COLARDA

Hi there sun worshipping drinking buddies. Here we are for another fantastic report on a fabulous location that the corporation keep giving to us as a freebie, which we cannot believe, but cheers easy.

This time round it's an absolute classic. The fantastic Tradagon resort of Las Vegas in the Whoopie desert.

 Well first things first,
 After a very smooth flight thanks to Whippet Airlines, we arrived late at night at our fabulous hotel in the resort. Where we hit the bar, got off with a couple of waiters and had a good 3 nodes of sleep before thinking about making some delicious breakfast.

Here we are in the Hotel's amazing kitchen where they allow you to make your own pancakes. Of course ours were

doused in Tequilla and Pina Colarda. Completely lush....

A couple of excursions were laid on for us, courtesy of the resort. Firstly we experienced the delights of a Hump fluffle ride in the desert. Not only was this a great way to see the sights, but also, the saddle rubs against your twadge, making it even more pleasurable.

After this we were treated to a Whirly Flapper ride through the Grand Crevis. Wow, what an experience that was. We nearly flan shittled ourselves.

We were then shown the amazing beach around the Vegas Lake. The sand was golden and the warm water hosted a selection of water sports. We could not resist a ride on the giant Curve dangler, and managed to hang on for quite a while before slipping off.

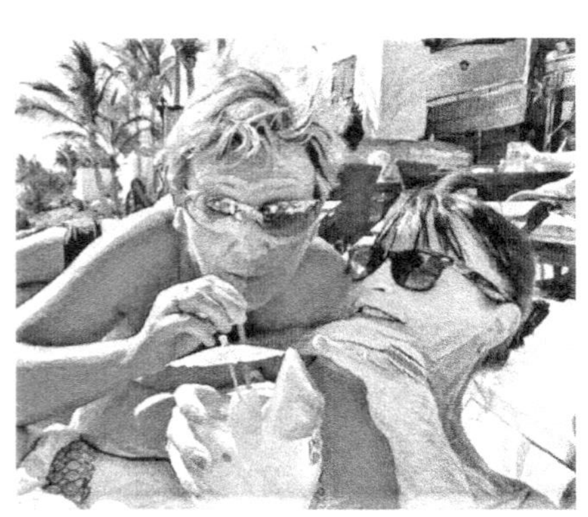

After all that excitement it was back to the pool to top up our tans and get smashed off our bongos on Tequilla and Pina Coladas.
We cannot recommend this trip enough. Till next time, Enjoy !!

MAUD
BABYSITTING

**She never brushes or flosses
And has so much food stuck
in her teeth that her breath is
perfect for children who
won't go to sleep.**

**All she has to do is breathe on them and they are
out for the count, sleeping soundly till the next
morning or even the following afternoon.
      Maud can even be hired for private Adult
parties to play the game 'Who am I?'
She simply breathes directly into your face and
you have 20 seconds to remember who you are.**

So Call Now ON   276 FACEFUMER for details.

SWELL GUY
BY SHOOT THEM UP LTD

Tired of being short?
Want to grow to your full
potential?
Then Try Swell Guy.
Simply pour some of the
Swell Guy solution into a
bowl of warm water and
stand in it for 2 nodes a
day. Within a week you'll
see the difference.

A side benfit of course is that not only do you
grow taller, but also your Ram dangler can
increase by a third. Pleasing your partner too !!

Just Call today for a trial sample on :-

784 LANKYBIGNOB

TRADAGON **HOROSCOPES** With Negative Nelly.

ARIES - You will produce your best fart Today. New pants required.

TAURUS - Venus has entered Uranus, I'd buy some
Lube if I were you.

GEMINI - Say yes to music but no to that pervy neighbour

CANCER - Take that special picture, but for fuck Sake don't show
Your parents.

LEO - You have thoughts of exercise today, don't fucking bother.

VIRGO - A painful tooth will lead to you punching your Gran.

LIBRA - Stop waiting for that bus, you own a car, you prick.

SCORPIO - Do what you want, it will fucking fail anyway.

SAGITTARIUS - An old man will shit on your lawn today.

CAPRICORN — A real joker in your life gets his head kicked in.

AQUARIUS — If single, love is in the air, if Married, wank.

PISCES - Hiding your emotions is cool, but you'll die alone.

SEBASTIAN HEADLINE
<u>WORDSEARCH</u>

Find The Following Words in the Grid Below:

Bongo, Fartel, Grollysquat, Wobbler, Plopper, Nudelites, Wajpizzle, Nudgewizzler, Twadge, Klunge pole, Flapper, Scringe, Beanbag, *Bonus word* – Shat.

```
T A U Q S Y L L O R G N
E W P L O P P E R A U G
L T C T W A D G E D P A
O E U K A C S O G N O B
P O G L J R F E P U Z N
E J W N P X W U H D R A
G F O V I I D Y K E X E
N A B U Z R L Q P L N B
U R B Z Z H C P W I A G
L T L G L O A S V T P J
K E E M E L D W N E O W
R L R N F N T A H S C T
```

Thank You Earthlings For Visiting My Newsroom. Who Knows We May Well Meet Again.

The Doubtful Tale Series
By
Mark Fribbens

cvdarts@hotmail.com
www.cvdarts.com

 **Cvd Arts**

We very much hope you enjoyed
This publication and please look
Out for further 'Doubtful Tales'
Coming soon.

CVD Creative Arts Publishing
Copyright 2021 Mark Fribbens

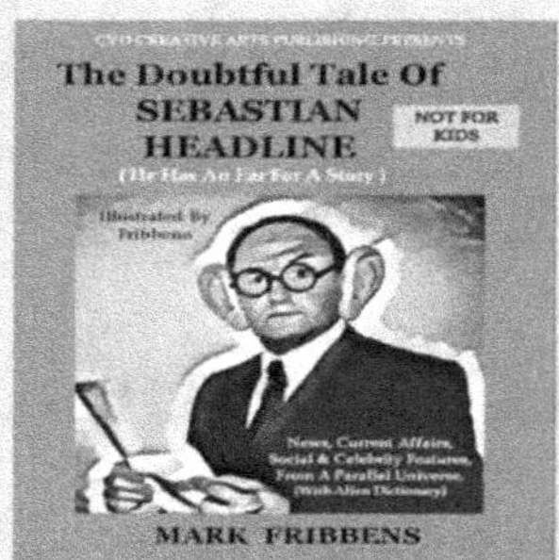

Also Available in 2021

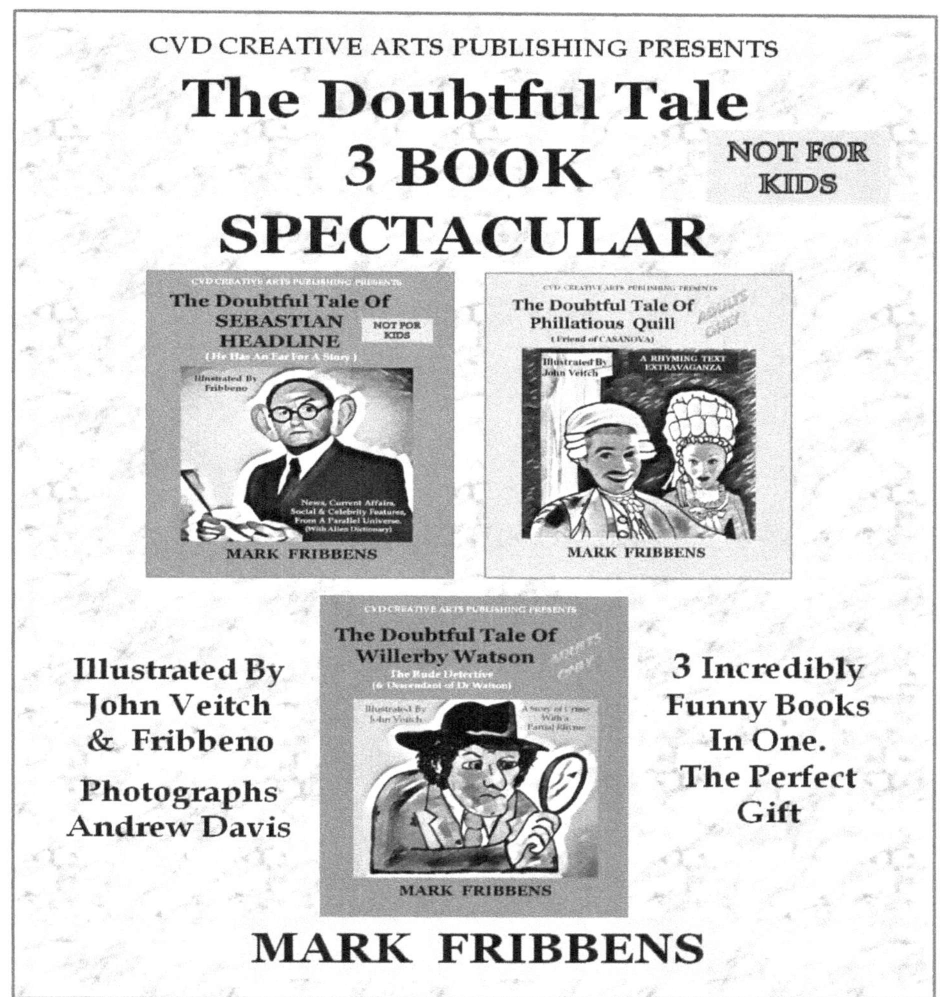

To Keep up to date with 'The Doubtful Tales' Info, simply E-mail your details to markfribbensauthor@gmail.com

TRADAGON - ENGLISH
<u>DICTIONARY</u>

Baker Box - Oven

Bean Bags - Nuts

Bee Splurge - Honey

Bongos - Tits

Bongo Sling - Bra

Bot Bazooka - Loud and smelly fart

Bot Snugglers - Underwear

Bugger Box - Bumhole (politician's)

Burple - Simmer

Carniboshers - Butchers

Churney - Butter

Clear juice - Water

Cluck orbs - Eggs

Comodal - Tin

Crackers - Testicles

Crevis - Canyon

Curve Dangler - Banana

Dipping your schnoozle - Freeing your imagination

Eye hedges - Eyebrows

Fartel - Boil

Five ring festival - The Olympics

Flabbage - Fat

Flan shittled - crapped

Flappage - Wings

Flapper - Bird

Fleshty - Skin

Gilly slip - Fish

Grill - Face

Grill poker - Beak

Grollysquat - Vegetable

Hump Fluffle - Camel

Klunge - Fanny

Klunge flaps - Labia

Klunge Pole - Dildo

Kniffle - Knife

Melodic bounce station - Nightclub

Nobblers - Bouncers

Nodes   -   Hours

Nookies   -   Amateurs

Nosebag   -   Lunch

Nudelites   -   Streakers

Nudge Wizzlers   -   Nipples

Pecker   -   Hen or Chicken

Peepers   -   Eyes

Plopper   -   Pan

Plops   -   Wickets

Pod rollers   -   Peas

Pop on the nob   -   Corn on the cob

Puss Podule   -   Spot

Ram dangler   -   Penis

Redbot fluff mongler   -   Baboon

Rhyme   -   Thyme

Sawty   -   Salt

Schnozzles   -   Carrots

Scringe   -   Strain

Scrumpy juice   -   Cider

Shat   -   Scum

Shitlet   -   small amount of crap

Shoo leads   -   Laces

Siren Bobby Men   -   Police

Sniffer   -   Rabbit

Splodge   -   Oil

Sprodget   -   Hairy, Curvy, Tradagon Creature

Stick toppers   -   Bails

Sweet grain   -   Sugar

Tattage   -   Potatoes

Tongue tizzle   -   Snog

Twadge   -   Female genitalia

Twizzler _   Spicy

Waj Pizzle   -   Clove

Wam Schniggler   -   Wild Pig

Wimple Tube   -   Breathing pipe

Wang rubber   -   Wanker

Whirly flapper   -   Helicopter

Wobbler   -   Mound of flesh

Wrinkler   -   Pensioner

DOUBTFUL TALES DOUBTFUL TALES

DOUBTFUL TALES DOUBTFUL TALES

DOUBTFUL TALES DOUBTFUL TALES

DOUBTFUL TALES DOUBTFUL TALES

DOUBTFUL TALES DOUBTFUL TALES

DOUBTFUL TALES DOUBTFUL TALES

DOUBTFUL TALES DOUBTFUL TALES

DOUBTFUL TALES DOUBTFUL TALES

DOUBTFUL TALES DOUBTFUL TALES

DOUBTFUL TALES DOUBTFUL TALES

DOUBTFUL TALES DOUBTFUL TALES

DOUBTFUL TALES DOUBTFUL TALES

DOUBTFUL TALES DOUBTFUL TALES

DOUBTFUL TALES DOUBTFUL TALES

DOUBTFUL TALES DOUBTFUL TALES
DOUBTFUL TALES DOUBTFUL TALES
DOUBTFUL TALES DOUBTFUL TALES
DOUBTFUL TALES DOUBTFUL TALES
DOUBTFUL TALES DOUBTFUL TALES
DOUBTFUL TALES DOUBTFUL TALES
DOUBTFUL TALES DOUBTFUL TALES
DOUBTFUL TALES DOUBTFUL TALES
DOUBTFUL TALES DOUBTFUL TALES
DOUBTFUL TALES DOUBTFUL TALES
DOUBTFUL TALES DOUBTFUL TALES
DOUBTFUL TALES DOUBTFUL TALES
DOUBTFUL TALES DOUBTFUL TALES
DOUBTFUL TALES DOUBTFUL TALES